STARRING

Jules

(AS HERSELF)

BETH AIN

Illustrated by Anne Keenan Higgins

Scholastic Press / New York

★ ★ ★

Library of Congress Cataloging-in-Publication Data

Ain, Beth Levine.
Starring Jules (as herself) / Beth Ain; illustrated by Anne Keenan Higgins.
p. cm.
Summary: Jules is an ordinary seven-year-old girl, concerned with school and friends and other ordinary things — until a chance meeting with a casting director leads to an audition for a television commercial.
ISBN 978-0-545-44352-4
1. Acting — Auditions — Juvenile fiction. 2. Friendship — Juvenile fiction. 3. Elementary schools — Juvenile fiction. [1. Acting — Fiction. 2. Auditions — Fiction. 3. Friendship — Fiction. 4. Elementary schools — Fiction. 5. Schools — Fiction.] I. Higgins, Anne Keenan, ill. II. Title.
PZ7.A277St 2013
813.6 — dc23
2012017678

Designed by Natalie C. Sousa

12 11 10 9 8 7 6 5 4 3 2   13 14 15 16 17 18/0

Printed in the U.S.A.   23
First printing, March 2013

for
GRACE EDEN
and
ELIJAH HENRY
(as themselves)

CONTENTS

fizzy milk, to-do lists, and promising maybes

"That's how you make a fizzy ice-cream cone / That's how you do it / That's how you do it." I look up from my cup full of milk bubbles and see my little brother, Big Henry, eyeing me.

"What's a fizzy ice-cream cone?" Henry asks.

"It's a milk cup full of bubbles," I say, blowing into my straw and humming my jingle.

"I want one!" Henry yells.

"You want what?" the waitress asks. She's been hovering since my mom went to the restroom. "You want an imaginary ice-cream cone?"

"Yeth," Henry says to the waitress.

"You want one?" I ask. "No problemo." I pour my mom's ice water into my brother's ice water and then pour half my milk into the empty cup. *Voilà!* I look up and the waitress has walked away from us. I think she thought I couldn't take care of my little brother all by myself while my mom was in the restroom, but she was wrong. I can take care of him just fine. I poke a straw in his cup and hand it over. "Here you go, Big Henry."

Henry looks at the cup of bubbles with big eyes and blows into the straw. I join him and get back to humming my jingle.

"Jules!" My mom is back. By now, our fizzy ice-cream cones are up to our eyebrows.

"What?" I say into my straw. I laugh when I see that this makes even more bubbles.

"Whoa! Not funny, Jules," she says.

"Then why are you smiling?" I ask.

"Because it's a little bit funny," she says, sitting down.

"It is, right?" I say.

"Yes, it is," she says. "Now stop it."

"Yes, ma'am," I say.

"Big Henry," I tell my brother, "that's enough, now. We have to make a list."

"Of what?" Henry asks.

"Of things to do before I turn eight," I say.

"Mommy," I say, "pen, please!"

"Yes, ma'am," she says, handing over a pen with a turquoise felt tip. My mom and I have a lot in common, including:

1. Loving the color turquoise more than any other color.

2. Loving lists.

Things to Do Before I Turn Eight, I write on a napkin.

1. Finish fizzy ice-cream cone jingle.

2. Be perfect at performing fizzy ice-cream cone jingle.

3. Find a new best friend since Charlotte Stinkytown Pinkerton has turned out to be the worst best friend ever.

"Jules," my mom says, "why'd you write that about Charlotte?"

"Because it's true," I say. "I can't believe she was ever my best friend in the first place. How could you have let that happen?" I ask.

"Because it was nursery school and you and Charlotte loved each other," my mom says.

"What did I love about her? Her pink sparkly barrettes? Her pink sparkly tights? Her pink sparkly backpack?"

My mom sighs really loud now.

"What?" I ask.

"I never know how you're going to feel about Charlotte on any given day," she says. "Tomorrow, you will probably love her again. And Abby and Brynn, too."

"No way, José," I say. "Any person who can just go off on a big fancy vacation and come back with fancy fingernails and two new best friends . . . well, we will never, not ever, be best friends again."

"Oh, it was the vacation," my mom says. "I see. The one they all went on together."

"At the place with the towels," I say.

"The towels." My mom says this and puts down her menu.

I can tell that this means that she needs me to explain. "You know, where they lay out the towels on your pool chair like maybe you don't have arms or something, and it's all because they just want to be as fancy as they can be and not because any-one needs to have their towels laid out for them," I say.

"Well, *I* would like that," Big Henry says now.

"No you would not, Big Henry, because there are kids who are starving," I say.

"Where?" he says.

"In the world," I say.

"*I'm* starving," he says right now.

I am too upset to even have an answer for this.

"Well, anyway," my mom says, "I thought all of you were best friends. You and Charlotte and Abby and Brynn. If you're not friends with any of them anymore, who's left?" she asks.

"Teddy!" Big Henry shouts.

I snort some milk bubbles into my cup at this.

"What?" my mom asks. "You and Teddy are meant to be."

"Jules!" I hear my dad's voice.

"Oh, thank goodness you're here," I say. "Mommy thinks I ought to be best friends with Stinkytown and also that I'm meant to be with Teddy Lichtenstein." I pause. "Teddy. Lichtenstein." I say it again — slowly, for emphasis.

"Well, I think you ought to clean up that snorted milk," he says, smiling.

"Daddy!" Big Henry says, standing right up in the booth and stepping his giant four-year-old sneaker right into the middle of the table before throwing himself into my dad's arms.

"Big Henry!" my dad says.

"Want to hear my jingle?" I ask, mopping up my milk.

"Does it have to do with fizzy ice-cream cones?" my dad asks.

"Mmm-hmm," I say.

"Then yes," he says.

I clear my throat and let my best jingle voice out. "That's how you make a fizzy ice-cream cone / That's how you do it / That's how you do it."

I feel people's eyes on me and my face gets hot.

"Don't stop," a woman says. She is sitting in the booth behind us.

"Sorry," I say, turning around.

"Yes," my mom says. "Don't mind us. You know how it is."

"Yes," the woman says, "I do." Then she stands up and comes around to our side of the booth. I look up at her and see that she is beautiful. Movie-star beautiful. She has long red hair and long feather earrings on and her eyes are sparkly and green.

"My name is Colby Kingston," she says, looking at me and not at my mom or dad, "and I was sitting there thinking, Who is this kid with all that pizzazz at the next table?"

Pizzazz? I think to myself. Now there's a word that belongs on my list of possible signature words.

"And then I heard her sing and, well, she's got quite a voice."

Now it is my mom who clears her throat. "Hi," she says, shooting her hand out at the woman for a shake, "I'm Rachel Bloom, and this is my husband, Robby. And these two are Henry —"

"Big Henry," I say.

"Big Henry," my mom continues, "and Jules."

"Well, all I can say is that I find all of you, well . . . entertaining," she says. And then she says something else. "Especially Jules."

My face goes from hot to on fire, and I wonder if Colby Kingston notices, and then I wonder if she will take back all the nice things she's been saying about me, since a person with pizzazz probably does not get an on-fire face in a situation like this. I picture a nice, calm, grown-up type of person taking these compliments and smiling and shaking hands with Colby Kingston the way my mom did and saying things like, *"Isn't this place just great? The scrambled eggs and chocolate milk are especially delicious here. Definitely better than that other diner. Hm? Yes, I know, too crowded."* And then I think that this imaginary person has pizzazz, not me.

"Well, anyway," I hear her saying, "here's my card. Please give this a shot. It's just not every day you come across someone like her."

I think maybe Colby Kingston is talking about me, but I'm not sure because I was too busy thinking about my hot face and scrambled eggs and chocolate milk while she was talking to my parents. "See you soon, Jules. Bye, Big Henry!" And just like that, she is gone.

"Well, what do you think of that?" my dad says.

"Of what?" I say.

"Of auditioning for a TV commercial," my mom says. "It's flattering, Julesie, but I don't —"

"Wait, what?" I say.

"Didn't you hear what she said?" my dad asks.

"I was thinking about something else," I say.

"Well, she's a casting director and she thinks you are just right for a kids' mouth-wash commercial," my mom says, waving a little card all around. "That's what you missed while you were out."

"While you were out" is my mom's way of saying "While you were daydreaming and inventing a completely different universe from the one we are currently living in."

"Is Jules going to be on TV?" Big Henry asks.

"Am I?" I ask.

"We'll have to think about it," my dad says.

"Wait," my mom says. "Would you even want to do something like this, Jules?"

I can't think of the right answer.

"Wow," my dad says. "She's speechless. Let's get that Colby Whatever-Her-Last-Name-Is back here. Maybe she can get you to go to bed on time, too."

"Colby Kingston," I say. And then I say, "Yes."

"Yes, what?" my mom asks.

"Yes, I'd like to be on a TV commercial," I say.

My mom and dad look at each other and I think they are going to say no because that's what usually happens when they look at each other before answering.

I cover my ears.

"It isn't a no, Jules," my dad says, laughing.

"It's a maybe," my mom says.

"I'll take a maybe," I say.

Maybe is the most exciting word I've heard since *pizzazz*.

TAKE TWO

yeps, nopes, and sweatshirts from far-off places

I blink my eyes open and a list pops right into my head.

Things I Would Change About My Room:

1. It would be all turquoise instead

of all yellow since turquoise makes me think of the ocean in Florida and yellow makes me think of dog pee on white snow.

2. It would have Christmas lights strung up all around because twinkly lights make everything look better, even my bulldog, Ugly Otis.

3. It would be all mine.

"Time to huthle, Jules." My lispy room-mate, Big Henry, is nose-to-nose with me. He thinks the closer he gets to my face, the more likely I am to listen to him.

"Ready," I say, and then I pull the covers up over my face and hide. Big Henry helps me by dragging me off the bed by my feet until I hit the floor with a thud. "Henry!" I shout, but I cannot be mad because I am laughing too hard.

"Are you up now?" my mom asks from the doorway.

"Uh, yes," I say from the floor. "I'm up, all right."

I think it is a day for layering and light-up high-top sneakers, so it takes me an extra five minutes to get ready. I put on a blue-and-white-striped long-sleeve shirt, which means I have to put on my violet corduroy overall shorts — the ones with red poppies all over them — which means I have to put on my navy tights with the turquoise polka dots, because I can only wear my poppy overall shorts with my polka-dot tights. Then I remember that it is March, and even though March seems like it might be a springtime month, it mostly feels like a wintertime month, so I pull on my argyle kneesocks because they will keep my shins warm when the wind blows. And also because I love to say *argyle*.

Out in the hallway, standing in front of the elevator, my mom shoves a blueberry waffle into my hand as the doors open and I fake-smile at all the people dressed in business suits. Outside, the city is wide awake. The air is cool and damp, and the flowers at the corner market have little droplets on them.

"It's gonna be a fun day, huh, Jules?" my mom asks.

"Yep," I say. I am not good at listening in the morning. Things like minivan taxis and women in high heels clickety-clacking on the street distract me.

"Are you excited to meet the new girl?"

"Yep," I say.

"Excited for your audition?"

"Yep," I say. "Hey!"

"What?" my mom asks with a big old smile on her face.

"I get to go?" I ask.

"Yep," she says.

"Today?" I ask.

"Nope," she says. "Friday, right after school."

I haven't breathed a breath since she said I could go, so I finally exhale. Today is Tuesday. That gives me four full school days to think about having the perfect pizzazz-ful audition. That ought to be enough time.

"Why didn't you tell me?" I ask.

"I'm telling you right now," she says. "Daddy and I called Colby Kingston last night and she told us she was looking forward to seeing you again."

"Pizzazz," I say out loud.

"What?" she says.

"Nothing," I say. But all I think the whole bus ride to school is *pizzazz, pizzazz, pizzazz, pizzazz,* and I picture that scrambled-eggs-and-chocolate-milk version of myself walking into the audition with sunglasses and a tall icy drink because it seems that people like that are always sucking on straws attached to tall icy drinks. I think that this tall-icy-drink person would do just fine in a minty-mouthwash commercial.

I am only distracted by this news for a little while since, thankfully, today is the day we are getting a new student in our class — a girl from London! Her name is Elinor and from the minute I heard about

her, I just knew Elinor of London was going to be my new best friend.

And it's about time. I've been waiting for a new best friend since January 3rd, when Stinkytown decided to turn into a pink sparkly blob of a boss instead of a regular seven-year-old girl. And now it has been a whole entire two months of watching Charlotte and Brynn and Abby poke each other in the ribs at things I don't understand, whispering secrets they probably learned at that fancy resort hotel. Secrets they probably can't tell me because nobody lays out your towels for you at the Museum of Natural History, which is where I spent most of my winter break. And two whole months of listening to them call themselves the ABC's: Abby. Brynn. Charlotte. There are six letters in between *Charlotte* and *Jules*, but there might as well be one hundred. *Fingers crossed for Elinor of London*, I think, walking into my classroom.

The very first thing we do at school, after we hang up our backpacks and sit down at our desks, is freewriting. We are supposed to take five minutes to put our thoughts on paper so we can clear our minds for the day. No matter how much freewriting I do, my mind will never be clear, which is why I keep lists. Today, I can't do anything but tap my pencil over and over and over while we wait. I can only think about my audition and meeting my new best friend. I try again to write something down.

Things I Will NOT Do at My Audition:

1. Burp into the microphone when I mean to sing into the microphone.

"What audition?" Charlotte whispers.

"Charlotte!" I whisper back. "You looked at my page."

"So?" she asks. "Was it a secret? If it was a secret, you should have guarded it with your arm, like this." Charlotte puts her arm around her own page and buries her face inside it.

"Well, I didn't think anyone would be peeking at my work," I say. I always wish I could think of just the right thing to say to make Charlotte stop talking like she knows everything, but I never, ever can. Even when we were friends, I used to wish this. I bet the tall-icy-drink-drinking person would know what to say.

"So, what audition, Jules?" Charlotte demands. "You know, my uncle is a big Hollywood director and he's going to make me a star one day. You could be, too, if you would just dress like a girl and smile more."

"I smile plenty," I say, but what I can't help thinking about is Hollywood. My grandma Gilda lives in Hollywood and when we go down to Florida to visit her, I mostly eat deli sandwiches and watch old ladies play cards on the beach. I don't know how a person would get to be famous there. "And besides, I do dress like a girl. Look," I say, pointing to my navy blue tights with turquoise polka dots all over them.

"Tights aren't girly when you wear them under overall shorts with high-top sneakers, Jules." Then Charlotte smiles at me the way a person does when they don't mean to smile at all. What they mean is that they don't want to be talking to you at all anymore, so they smile in a way that ends the conversation. I am familiar with this because I am usually the one who smiles this way at Charlotte.

"Fine," I say.

"Fine," she says back.

"Girls! Do I need to separate you?" Ms. Leon asks from her desk.

Yes, I think. *Please, please, please separate us.* But she does not. I forgive Ms. Leon for this because she is the best teacher I have ever had. She is from Cuba and her English sounds like the music they play on the beach in Florida.

"Okay, ev-er-ee-body," Ms. Leon says, standing up from her desk, "penceels down. Any minute, Eleenor will be here with us and we are going to welcome her with open arms!" And just like that, the door swings open and there she is. Elinor of London. In my head, I say this with a British accent to make it sound more important. *Elinoh of Lohndon.*

As Ms. Leon shows Elinor to her desk, I notice she is wearing a turquoise sweatshirt that says *I Heart Roma* on it, and even though I don't know exactly what that means, I smile at her. It is turquoise, after all. Elinor smiles back. *Best friends forever,* I think.

"Jules, will you show Elinor around the school for a few minutes during recess?" Ms. Leon asks.

"Sure," I say calmly. Inside, I do a backflip.

"And Charlotte, you help, too," Ms. Leon says.

I fall on my head mid-backflip.

"Yay!" Charlotte says, clapping.

☆　☆　☆　☆　☆

When recess comes, I walk right over to Elinor. I want to say, *"Hi, Elinor, I am your new best friend forever, Jules."* Instead, I say, "Hi, Jules. I'm Elinor." Yes, this is what I say.

"Oh. My. Goodness," Charlotte says. "Jules, you are a real doof!"

My face heats up and I get a lump in my throat the size of a hard-boiled egg. But just when I think I'm going to throw up egg salad all over Elinor's shoes, she says, "Hi, Elinor. I'm Jules." Charlotte looks at her like she's crazy and all I can do is laugh.

"So nice to meet you, Jules," I say. "What a great name you have."

"You think so?" she asks in the prettiest accent I have ever heard. Then she says, "I like yours so much better." But when she speaks it sounds like this: "I like yaws so much bettah." Amazing.

"Great," Charlotte says. "Another Jules."

"Let's go," I say. "I'll show you where the least smelly girls' bathroom is."

"Lovely," Elinor says. I start a list in my head.

Things I Love About My New Best Friend:

1. She says lovely when everyone else would just say great.

After we walk Elinor all around the school, we head outside to the playground. "Elinor, why don't you come and do makeovers with the ABC's?" Charlotte asks. "I have fruit-flavored lip gloss." This is how Charlotte has changed. She went away on an airplane to some fancy-schmancy hotel and came back with sparkly pens and flavored makeup. And it isn't that she didn't always like fancy things a little more than I like fancy things. It's just that she used to also like normal things, like swing sets and Cheerios.

"Makeovers?" I say. "We're going to dig for worms."

"We are?" Elinor asks.

"I mean, if you want to," I say. This is what Teddy and I do at recess these days. Yes, I have resorted to playing with Teddy Meant-to-Be Lichtenstein at recess. I have known Teddy since we were exactly two-and-a-half years old. According to my mom and Teddy's mom (who have been best friends ever since

Teddy and I were assigned cubbies right next to each other on the first day of nursery school) he would give me a big kiss on my cheek every single morning of that terrible-twos program. Here is my list of things you need to know about Teddy:

1. Teddy is much too smart for his own good.

2. Teddy and I really don't have anything in common at all except:

   a. brunch (which we have to have together about once

a month because our parents like to talk to each other while waiting in long lines for multigrain pancakes when we could just be eating Multi Grain Cheerios in a Sunday-morning fort in the living room).

b. our (brilliant!) worm-swimming-pool idea.

3. Teddy is very good at dealing with worms and very bad at dealing with seven-year-old people.

"It is primo worm-digging season and we want to build a worm swimming pool," I explain to Elinor.

"Primo?" Charlotte asks, narrowing her eyes at me. "Did you say *primo* because of the *I Heart Roma* sweatshirt?"

I have no idea what Charlotte is talking about. *Primo* is a word my dad uses a lot and one I love. It is on my list of potential signature words. Elinor chuckles at this and I make a note to ask my parents what *primo* has to do with *Roma*.

"You don't want to play with Teddy," Charlotte says to Elinor.

"Why, what's wrong with Teddy?" Elinor asks.

"Everything," Charlotte says.

"Oh, don't listen to her," I say. "She's just mad that Teddy doesn't like her enough to give her an element name."

"As in, the Periodic Table of Elements?" Elinor asks.

"Yes," I say. "Whatever that is, Teddy is obsessed with it."

"Julesium!" Teddy is running toward us, and Charlotte braces herself.

To me, Teddy is kind of like a bouncing Super Ball. The kind that bounces so high and crazy you have to cover your head once you've let it go just so it doesn't hit you when you aren't looking. Right now, the bouncing ball is coming right for Charlotte, and Teddy bumps right into her as he comes to a stop.

"Ow!" she says.

"Sorry, Charlotte," he says, looking horribly worried.

"It's okay," I say. "Charlotte will live. Just don't throw up." Elinor looks at me. Something I left off the list:

4. Even though I always think I'm going to throw up all over the place, Teddy actually does.

Teddy swallows hard. I suspect he has swallowed throw up. "Who's this?" he asks.

"This is Elinor," I say.

"Pleased to meet you, Teddy," she says, shaking his hand. Elinor reminds me of my mother and Colby Kingston when she does this.

"Go and dig for worms, if you want," Charlotte says, rubbing her arm dramatically. "When you get tired of being with the weirdos, come play makeover with us."

"We'll save some mud for you," I say. "It's supposed to be good for your face." Judging from her squinty eyes, Charlotte doesn't think this is funny.

"Thanks very much for everything, Charlotte," Elinor says.

I add another item to my list of things I like about my new best friend:

2. Speaks in complete sentences, even when talking to Stinkytown.

"The ABC's?" Elinor asks, turning to Teddy and me.

"Abby, Brynn, Charlotte," I say.

"It's alphabetical," Teddy says.

"It's ridiculous," I say, and hope Elinor agrees.

"Charlotte used to be Julesium's best friend," Teddy says. I am so mad that I give Teddy a push. Not too hard a push because it's Teddy, but still. The boy needs to be pushed for what he has just told my new best friend.

"And so, if I play with you, I am one of the weirdos, as Charlotte calls you?" Elinor asks.

"That's right," I say.

"True," Teddy agrees.

We all look at each other for a minute, until at last Elinor says, "All right, then, worms with weirdos it is!"

"All right!" I say, beaming. Somehow, Elinor has turned Charlotte's fruit-flavored insult into a compliment, which gets me to thinking about what else this girl can do with her excellent manners and her especially excellent turquoise *I Heart Roma* sweatshirt.

TAKE THREE

boys in helmets, minty-fresh mysteries, and the writing on the wall

"I have some important questions," I say to my mom while she makes dinner. For my mom, making dinner means shaking some cheese over pasta while she dashes in and out of what used to be the pantry, but is now her painting studio. She uses canned goods in her art *and* in her cooking. My mom, Rachel Bloom, is a much better artist than a cook, and I know this because her art hangs in a gallery where there is a sign in the window that says, FEATURING THE WORKS OF MIXED-MEDIA ARTIST RACHEL BLOOM. No one would ever put a sign like that over her pasta and broccoli.

"Shoot," she says.

I raise my hand.

"Yes, Jules?" my mom asks in a teacher voice.

"Mrs. Bloom," I say. I like pretending that my mom is the teacher. "What is *Roma* and what does it have to do with the word *primo*?"

"*Roma* is the Italian word for Rome, which is a city in Italy, and *primo* means 'prime' in Italian. *Prime*, as in 'excellent, the best, first-class'! Very good questions, Jules."

"Ohhhh," I say. I hate it when Charlotte knows something I don't.

"Why?" she asks.

"Elinor of London was wearing an *I Heart Roma* sweatshirt."

"Elinor!" my mom says. "I completely forgot to ask about her. Is she great? New-best-friend material?"

"She really is. She's perfect. She says *lovely* and shakes people's hands and speaks in complete sentences."

"Did you start a list?" my mom asks.

"Yes," I say, "and her sweatshirt is turquoise, not gray like my *I Heart* NY t-shirt."

"Wow," she says. "She *is* perfect."

"Big Henry!" my little brother says, gliding into the living room on his bright orange scooter. He announces himself whenever he enters a room, even if he has only been gone for a second. He is wearing his dinosaur pajamas and a helmet with ears on it.

"Big Henry!" my dad says, walking through the front door at that very instant and scooping up my little brother. "Look what I have," he says, waving a piece of paper in his hand.

"What is it?" I ask. My dad is a chef at a restaurant, which means he is not usually home for dinner. But right now, he is in the middle of opening his own restaurant, a restaurant that has all organic food, which means it will be a healthy and delicious restaurant. But — and this is a big but — it is for now a restaurant that no one can think of a name for, and a restaurant that does not yet have any tables or chairs inside, so for now, he is home every single night for dinner, just like in a regular family.

He hands me the mystery piece of paper.

I look at the paper.

Swish Mouthwash for Kids, script

"Whoa," I say. "Minty." I picture myself wrapped in a winter scarf and wearing mittens and I am going to sled all the way down the hill into Riverside Park on a massive snow slope. This is what mint reminds me of — sledding. And also chocolate mint candies, which are the best candies ever invented. So good, I don't know why anyone would eat M&M'S when they could be eating chocolate mint candies instead.

"Whoa, minty," Big Henry says, jumping up and down next to me. Having Big Henry for a little brother is like having an echo. A not-so-good-at-standing-still echo.

I quickly turn the page over. "I'll look at it later," I say.

"Jules," my dad says, "you're going to need to practice before Friday."

"I will," I say.

"Voilà!" my mom says, plopping down a big bowl of whole-wheat bow-tie pasta mixed with broccoli and shaky cheese. I look at my dad. "What?" my mom asks. "It has all the things a person needs for dinner. Whole grains, cheese, and green vegetables."

"Sure," he says, "but the kids need to develop their palates." Both my parents talk about palates a lot, but when my dad says it, he means taste buds, and when my mom says it, she means colors. Sometimes, I wonder if they know they are not talking about the same thing.

I take a big bite of pasta and hand Ugly Otis a piece of broccoli under the table. He gobbles it up. He should be called Ugly Otis: The Broccoli-Loving Dog of the Universe, for all the broccoli he eats out of my hand.

"That's what you can call the restaurant," my mom says. "Palate." She puts her fork down then and stands up. We all look at her like she is going to make a big announcement, but she doesn't.

She just goes into her studio and returns with a paintbrush and a can of bright red paint. I watch her every move. When my mom gets an idea, it can be even better than watching a movie. She plops the little can down next to the white wall in the living room and my dad and I look at each other.

"What are you going to paint?" I ask.

"Restaurant name ideas," she answers, and then we all watch as she paints the word *Palate* on the wall in beautiful, swooping letters.

"Starlight Café!" I shout. I love this idea. I love every red inch of it.

"Just Good Food," my dad says.

"Robot!" Big Henry yells, bouncing. His eyes are all lit up.

My mom paints them all up there, one by one, and I feel my own eyes light up, too. This is going to make my list of my favorite things my mom has ever done.

Number one on that list is when she took me into a fountain in the middle of stinking hot Philadelphia when we were visiting my uncle last summer. Watching her paint words on the wall like this feels a lot like swimming in that city fountain with all of our clothes on.

☆ ☆ ☆

After homework and reading, I hop quietly into my bed. Big Henry is already asleep on the other side of the curtain that divides our room. My side of the curtain has ocean waves painted on it and Henry's looks like a nighttime sky. My mom flicks on the little reading light that clips on to my book and whispers, "Good night, Julesie. Don't stay up too long." I give her a kiss and a thumbs-up and she is gone. I can hear Big Henry's book on tape playing Paddington softly. I picture Elinor shaking Big Henry's hand and Big Henry falling over when he hears her Paddington Bear accent. *He is just going to love her,* I think. Then I pull out that piece of paper I am supposed to study.

There are a few lines I have to read before I swish some Swish Mouthwash in my mouth and say, *"And who wouldn't love that orange-fresh taste?"* After that, it says *smile,* which gets all blurry on the page when I read it because I am about to have a panic attack.

I sit straight up in bed. "Mom!" I scream at the top of my lungs, and then all I can hear is Big Henry waking up and crying and crying and crying.

"Jules!" my mom says.

"What on earth?" my dad says.

"It says orange," I say.

"What says orange?" my mom asks.

"This!" I wave the page around. My dad is holding Big Henry now and they are all on my side of the curtain.

"Well, do you have to taste it or do you just have to say it?" my mom asks.

"Take a big mouthful, blow out cheeks, swish it around, it says." I look back up at my parents and feel tears in my eyes.

"Okay, now, Jules. Just because you threw up one time a long, long time ago, that doesn't mean it will happen again," my dad says. "Besides, that was orange sherbert. This is orange mouthwash. The whole point of mouthwash is that you spit it out."

My dad has a point. Orange anything reminds me of throw up, partly because I threw up in a taxicab after eating that orange sherbert, and partly because I think everything orange is just plain terrible. Orange Tic Tacs, the orange t-shirts they made us wear every single day at camp,

★60★

and now orange mouthwash. I can't believe anyone on this planet would ever think this was a good idea.

"Jules, it's late. We'll deal with this in the morning," my mom says.

"Remember, every problem has a solution," my dad says.

"Is Jules going to throw up?" Big Henry asks.

"Not tonight, Hen," my dad says, and Henry closes his eyes.

I plop my head on my pillow and close my eyes and start a list in my head.

Solutions to the Anything-Orange-Makes-Me-Throw-Up Problem:

1. Blank.

2. Blank.

3. Blank.

I have no solutions. Not one. And then I think of Charlotte and her fruity lip gloss. There is probably an orange-flavored one and Charlotte must know how not to throw up from it. So now I just have to figure out how to ask Stinkytown for help.

the art of breathing,
the other Hollywood,
and things that make me itch

"Hi, Charlotte," I say, walking right up to the side of her desk with a big old fake smile on my face.

"Hi, Jules," she says, looking inside her desk for something and not seeing my fake smile.

"Hi, Julesium," Teddy says, too. I have to pass by his desk to get to Charlotte.

"Wait," Charlotte says, slamming down the lid of her desk, "what do you want?"

"I don't know what you mean," I say. I am trying out my acting skills. "I just wanted to say good morning to my long-lost best friend, Charlotte Stinky — er — Pinkerton." *Shoot*, I think. If I am going to be an actress, I have to get a whole lot better at acting.

"Aha!" she says. "You can't even pretend to be nice for one second, Jules Bloom, so just spit it out already. What do you want?"

"Do you have any orange-flavored lip gloss?" I ask.

Charlotte narrows her eyes at me. "I might," she says.

"Charlotte, do you or don't you?" I ask.

"I do. But what do you, the anti-lip-gloss-queen-of-the-worms, want with it?" she asks.

This is where I would normally end this conversation. But today, like it or not, I need Charlotte. "I need to practice trying it on and not throwing up."

"Mmm," Charlotte says. "It *is* a pretty pukey flavor." She puts her hand into her desk and pulls out the lip gloss, but stops short of handing it to me.

"So, why do you need to get used to orange-flavored anything?"

"Will you give it to me if I don't tell you?" I ask.

"No," she says. "I finally have something you want and you're finally talking to me, so no, I will not give it to you until you tell me more."

I *am finally talking to* her?

"Because she's auditioning for a big-time mouthwash commercial on Friday and the flavor of the mouthwash is orange and she once threw up in a taxi after eating orange sherbert and she's afraid she'll do it again."

"Teddy!" I am definitely going to be mad at my mom when I get home.

"What?" he says. "I'm trying to help you solve your problem, even though the real problem is that the company thinks any kid would want orange mouthwash."

"Forget that. How did *you* get an audition?" Charlotte asks, turning to me.

"Some lady came up to us at the diner the other night and asked my parents if I could do it," I say.

"Yes, I guess that's how people who aren't connected to Hollywood get auditions," she says.

"I'm connected to Hollywood," I say. "My grandma Gilda lives there." Charlotte snorts at this.

"Not Hollywood, *Florida*, Jules!" Then she starts laughing and laughing and laughing.

"Hollywood, *California*! Where all the big movies are made and where all the movie stars live and where you can put your knees right inside where Shirley Temple put her knees."

"Why would you do that?" Teddy asks.

"To see if you will be world famous, too," Charlotte says.

"Who says?" Teddy asks.

"I say!" Charlotte says. "Anyway, the point is, Jules doesn't know what Hollywood is!"

I feel my face get hot because everyone is laughing and it makes the room spin all around me.

★ 68 ★

"Well, I didn't know there were two Hollywoods in this country," Elinor says.

"You're new here, Elinor," Charlotte says. "Jules has lived here all her life."

"So, maybe Jules will get so famous, she'll make the other Hollywood world famous, too!" Elinor says.

This is where I would like to be the kind of person who gets all loud and says *"Yeah, what do you think about that, Stinkytown? Huh?"* But I am not. Even if I do get that commercial and do become a mouthwash-selling superstar, I will not be that person, or the scrambled-eggs-and-chocolate-milk person, or the tall-icy-drink person. I will still be the person who had the wrong Hollywood in the first place.

"Well, all I can say is that it's a good thing you told me about this, Jules. You need my help, don't you?" Charlotte asks.

I close my eyes and picture a person who does not need any help at all, and I see Colby Kingston. I am no Colby Kingston. I open my eyes, half hoping that the new Charlotte has gone away with a *poof!* and that the old Charlotte is standing before me, ready to play nice. But, no. The new, hands-on-her-hips Charlotte is still standing there waiting for me to answer. "Yes," I say.

"Okay, let's get to work. Today at recess. You, me, and a tube of orange lip gloss," she says.

"Okay," I say. "See ya."

"This is where you say 'Thank you, Charlotte,'" Charlotte says.

"Don't thank her yet," Teddy says. "Let's see if she can stop the puke first."

Charlotte glares at Teddy, and I sit down. Ms. Leon has cleared her throat and all I can think about now is that I forgot to say

thank you to Elinor for sticking up for me. I
pull out a piece of paper and scribble:

Dear Elinor,
   Thank you for sticking up for me,
even though I bet you <u>did</u> know that
there were two Hollywoods.
   Jules
   P.S. Want to come over after school
on Thursday?

I fold up my note into a teeny tiny square
and when Ms. Leon turns around to write
on the board, I pass it to Elinor.

She opens it right away, smiles big, and
mouths *yes*. *Thank goodness for Elinor*, I
think.

At recess, I meet Charlotte by the swing set, and so do Teddy and Elinor and the rest of the ABC's.

"Here." Charlotte thrusts the orange lip gloss in front of my nose and I feel my knees start to shake. There are only two times when my knees do this: when I think I might throw up and when I have to go up in front of the whole class to do a math problem or give a report or even if I only have to walk up and hand in something to Ms. Leon. Now that I think of it, this might be a good reason not to try and get famous, since most famous people have to stand in front of people a lot.

"Okay," Charlotte says. "Close your eyes and relax. We are going to do a for-real acting lesson. Take some deep breaths. Think of summertime and swing sets." When Charlotte says this it reminds me that she knows a lot about me.

I close my eyes and smell that smell that comes when winter is melting right off the swing set and into the ground. It smells like dirt and I start to picture myself digging for worms and then hoisting the fattest earthworm you ever saw into the air, then sending it flying off the highdive and into the worm swimming pool Teddy and I have built, and it

 all just seems so wonderful until I am rattled back to reality by new-Charlotte's yelling voice. Old-Charlotte only yelled things like *"Tag! You're it!"*

"Good!" Charlotte is saying. "Now focus, Jules. Focus on what I am saying. Pretend the lip gloss smells like your favorite food in the world." Even when she is cheerful, she still sounds so bossy.

"Meatballs?" I ask, squinting my eyes open.

Charlotte rolls her eyes at me.

"How about your favorite candy?"

"Black licorice?" I say.

"Why is it impossible for you to like any-thing normal?" Charlotte asks, throwing her hands in the air. I have to admit, she does seem like more of an actress than me.

"Well, then, you choose," I say.

"How about strawberries?" she asks.

"They give me a rash," I say.

"Peaches?"

"They make my lips swell up," I say.

"You know what?" Charlotte says. "I think you are kidding and that you are not at all allergic to those things. I think you just don't really want my help and what I think is that you are never going to get that com-mercial, Jules Bloom, and it serves you right, anyway, for dumping a superstar best friend like me in the first place."

"I did not dump you, Charlotte!" I say louder than I usually speak. "You dumped me when you and the ABC's started whispering to each other about fancy towels at fancy hotels, which is exactly when you started liking lip gloss more than swing sets!"

"Well, why didn't you just say that in the first place?!? And maybe you're the one who likes swing sets more than lip gloss, and who says that's better anyway?!" Charlotte shouts back. Then she stomps away, and Brynn and Abby follow.

I stare at her for a long time after she walks away, and even though she said a lot of things, I can only think about the part she said about me not getting the commercial.

"She's probably right," I say.

"About what?" Elinor asks.

"I won't get the commercial," I say.

"No way," Teddy says. "There has to be a scientific solution to this problem. I'll work on it and get back to you tomorrow."

"We'll figure it out, Jules," Elinor says. "I'm just excited that I've only lived in New York for a week and I already know an actress!"

"Who?" I ask. "Me or Charlotte?" At this, Teddy and Elinor crack up and we spend the rest of recess digging for worms that never come to the surface.

not-so-helpful science experiments, earth-rattling knees, and free-roaming relatives

Wednesday is a disaster so far.

List of Things That Have NOT Solved My Orange Problem:

1. Charlotte's for-real acting
   lesson.

2. Teddy's de-scents-itizing
   project. I don't exactly know
   what this means, but my mom
   called it this on our way home
   and I think it might be a clever
   mom joke, so I am using it on
   this list because I am too upset
   to think of a clever Jules way of
   describing Teddy's experiment.
   (Even though Teddy THOUGHT it
   would be a good idea to spray
   orange-scented air spray all
   over the classroom, it was very
   much NOT a good idea since it

made me think I was going to throw up in front of the whole class, which is a combination of the two things that make my knees shake the most, and therefore I had to run on wobbly legs to the nurse's office, where she had to call my mom just to calm me down, and now I am at home, feeling even more worried about my audition, which is the day after tomorrow.)

"Okay," my mom says. We are on the roof of our apartment building getting some fresh air. I feel like I can't get the smell of orange out of my nose, so my mom thinks this will help. "Let's figure this out."

"There's nothing to figure out," I say. "If I have to put that orange stuff in my mouth, it isn't going to be pretty. I guess this won't be my big break."

"Do you want it to be your big break?" my mom asks. "I didn't know you wanted to be an actress."

"Well, I kind of do," I say. "I love making up songs and performing them, I love pretending I'm someone else, and I love when people think I do a good job at those things. Like when you all clap and stand up and I get to take bows." I stop for a second. "There is one problem, though."

"What's that?"

"I only like doing those things in front of you and Daddy, and Big Henry."

"I see," she says.

"And actors are supposed to be loud and not afraid of people and not afraid of anything. Like Charlotte," I say.

"I think that's not really true," my mom says. "I think that's what people believe, but most actors are pretty shy, and the reason they like acting is because it's easier to be someone else in front of a crowd than it is to be themselves."

Sometimes my mom says things that confuse me and make me feel better at the exact same time. "Well, anyway," I say, "maybe we should call Colby Kingston and cancel."

"Hmmm," my mom says. "I think we should try one more thing."

She picks up her phone and dials. I can tell by all the numbers who she is calling. "Grandma Gilda!" I shout.

"Hi, Mom," my mom says into the phone. "Yes, mmm-hmmm, okay —" My grandma Gilda does a lot of talking right away and my mom does a lot of *trying* to talk. "Well, Jules has an audition on Friday and she's afraid of orange-flavored mouthwash —" She stops because she has been interrupted. I laugh and my mom holds out the phone while my grandma yells at her for not telling her sooner. She is

yelling so loud I can hear her from where I am sitting!

"Put Jules on," I hear through the phone.

"Grandma?" I say.

"Julesie," she says, "I am on my way." Click.

My mom looks at me. "She's on her way," I say. Then we both laugh. Only Grandma Gilda would say she's on her way when she lives all the way in Florida.

I have a list of things you need to know about Grandma Gilda.

1. She is the best thing since sliced cheese.

2. She's the one who taught me
   that expression, and she's also
   the one who taught me the
   word <u>expression</u>.

3. She lives on a street called
   Kokomo Key Lane, which sounds
   very much more special than West
   91st Street, which is why I spend
   a lot of time asking my parents
   why we can't move in with her.

4. She treats airplanes like buses
   and hops on the one that flies
   between Florida and New York
   City once a month.

5. She always tells me I have talent.
   (And I think she does not mean
   talent the way my parents mean
   it when they say I have a talent
   for pushing back bedtime in
   creative ways, like the Great
   Toothbrush Challenge between
   Big Henry and me, which I am
   currently winning, but which is
   getting seriously harder ever
   since my little brother started
   getting the hang of keeping
   the foaming toothpaste in his
   mouth longer and longer
   without dripping. Previously,
   this was something only I was

very good at.) Grandma Gilda
has said for a very long time
that my mom ought to put me
on television, as if a TV is
something you can just put
someone on.

Anyway, I suspect that Grandma Gilda is
packing her bags right this very second, as
my mom and I sit way up high over the city,
her soaking up the rooftop sun and me trying to blow that orange smell right out of
my nose and onto 91st Street.

"At least one good thing is going to happen tomorrow," I say.

"What's that?"

"Elinor of London is coming over!"

"Maybe she'll have a fresh idea for Daddy's restaurant," my mom says.

"Maybe she will," I say.

"FRESH!" my mom yells and runs over to the staircase door. *She is going to paint this on the wall,* I think. I run after her.

☆　☆　☆　☆　☆

Thursday at school, everyone is super nice to me instead of being super horrible to me about running out of the classroom with a green face and wobbly knees the day before.

"Sorry, Jules," Teddy says when he sees me.

"I was going to call you," Elinor says, "but I didn't have your information." I love that she calls my phone number my *information*. In my head, I add it to my Elinor list.

"I sure hope that isn't how you are planning to audition — by running out of the room with your hand over your mouth!" That is, everyone except Charlotte is super nice to me.

"We'll think of something this afternoon," Elinor says.

"It's useless," I say.

"Nope," Elinor says. "I promise you it isn't useless. I'm bringing my astrology book with me. My mom says you can figure out just about anything from the stars." I get

butterflies when she says this. I remind
myself that Elinor is the one who made
worms with weirdos sound like a nice thing
to say. Maybe there will be a solution
after all.

promising playdates,
spaghetti with peanut butter,
and other distractions

My dad and Big Henry pick us up from school today and we decide to walk the whole way home since it is so nice outside.

"Mr. Bloom," I say, raising my hand.

"Yes, Jules," my dad says in his best teacher voice, "what can I do for you?"

"How come it has been so sunny and warm and nice out, but there are no flowers and no worms yet?" I am frustrated that I haven't had my victory moment of hoisting up that big, fat earthworm and throwing him into our worm swimming pool.

"Well, what's the missing ingredient here?" he asks. My mom always says my dad could have been a scientist if he wasn't a chef. My dad says they are really the same thing.

"Is this a quiz?" I ask. I hate quizzes. They make me nervous.

"Rain," Elinor says.

"Ding, ding, ding!" my dad says.

"I told you she was smart," I say. "And she's got her astrology book with her today so we can get some answers from the stars."

"Astronomy," my dad says.

"Nope, astrology," I say.

"What's asthrology?" Big Henry asks.

"It's a bunch of hooey," my dad says.

"Hooey!" Big Henry says, flinging his head back from way up high on my dad's shoulders.

"Astronomy is the study of the planets and stars. Astrology is the study of how the planets and stars affect people's moods. One is science, the other is . . . Big Henry?"

"Hooey!" Big Henry says again.

"My mom says astrology can tell you a lot about yourself," Elinor says.

"And her mom is a professor," I tell my dad.

"Of what?" he says.

"Poetry," Elinor says. My dad just nods at this. I get the feeling he thinks astrology and poetry go together.

I feel a little nervous for the rest of the walk home because even though I usually love every little thing my dad says, I wish that maybe just this once he had not said that thing about astrology being hooey, since Elinor is my new best friend and I need her to keep being my new best friend since, when I really think about it, there is only one letter in between her and the ABC's.

☆ ☆ ☆ ☆ ☆

At home, Elinor and I race into my mom's studio so we won't be interrupted by Big Henry.

"Okay, Jules, what's your sign?" Elinor asks.

"I don't even know."

"When were you born?"

"July fifth," I say.

"Well, then you are a Cancer."

I gasp.

"You don't *have* cancer," Elinor says. "You are a Cancer — that means that your sign is Cancer — and it says here that you are creative, and my mom always says that we should go with what we know, so there's your answer."

"What's the answer?" I ask.

"You need to be creative," Elinor says. "Like when you said your name was Elinor and I said my name was Jules and we just went with it."

I love this idea. I don't know what it has to do with my audition and not throwing up, but I like that Elinor thinks I am the kind of person who can just go with it — whatever *it* is.

"What sign are you?" I ask.

"Oh, I'm a Virgo," she says. "It's an earth sign. I am very practical and orderly."

"Hmm," I say. "I think I'm neither of those things."

"You're not," she says. "You're a water sign."

"I am?" I picture the turquoise ocean. It all makes sense now.

"Yep."

"So, we're opposites?" I don't like this at all. Opposites is what Charlotte and I are.

One of us a digger of worms and the other a glosser of lips.

"Yep. Isn't that just perfect?" Elinor says. She's smiling, so I take this to mean that she is happy we are opposites.

"I guess," I lie. I picture us having a giganto-huge fight during a pretend game of family. In my head, it is a friendship-ending fight with lots of "*Well, I am a water sign and I want a family beach vacation,*" and then "*Well, I am an earth sign and I want to hike in the woods!*"

"Jules?" I hear Elinor's singsong voice come crashing through my day-mare. (*Day-mare* is what I call a scary daydream.)

"I think my dad is right," I say. "Astrology is a bunch of hooey." I run out of the pantry and into my room, where I belly flop my whole body onto the first bed I see. Big Henry's bed. I don't know why I do this or why I said that to Elinor, but I do know that I don't want to play with her too much because I might like her even more than I already do and then it will be even worse when we have that big argument.

"I'm Daddy," Big Henry says, standing at his play kitchen.

"What are you cooking, Hen?"

"Spaghetti," he says, "with peanut butter."

"Mmm," I say. "Delish."

"Where'th Elinor?" he asks.

"Elinor and I aren't going to be friends anymore," I say.

"Uh, Jules." My mom is standing in the doorway. "Come with me," she says.

"But I'm talking privately with Henry," I say.

"Now," she says. I follow her to her bedroom, where she pats the bed for me to sit next to her.

"What?" I ask.

"Well, I met Elinor just now. She is just as lovely as you said."

"I know this," I say.

"So then why did you run out on her?" she asks. "She said you made fun of the book she brought and that she wants to go home."

"I only said that because Elinor and I
won't agree on where our pretend family
will go on vacation," I say.

"You had an argument?"

"No," I say. "Not yet, but we will."

"Jules, what on earth?"

"We're opposites. She's an earth sign and very organized, and I'm a water sign and not at all organized, and that means we're opposites, just like Charlotte and I are opposites, and we all know how that turned out."

"You and Charlotte might be opposites, but the reason you aren't close is because you don't enjoy doing the same things anymore, which is okay. It is not because she went away on that beach vacation with the towels, you know. And for the record, not being close friends anymore doesn't mean that you can't still be nice to each other. As for you and Elinor, you both like astrology, right?"

"Yes," I say.

"And maybe she likes digging for worms with you, right? And you both definitely like turquoise — that much we know."

"So?"

"So, sometimes it's best to have someone who isn't exactly like you for a good friend. That way, when you are having wacky thoughts like you do, there will be someone around who isn't having such wacky thoughts to help you through it."

"You think I'm wacky?" I ask.

"Just a little," she says, "but in a good way."

"In a tall-icy-drink kind of way?" I ask.

"I don't know what that means," she says.

"Never mind," I say.

"Hey, maybe Elinor can help you organize your room," my mom says, smiling.

"And I can mess hers up?" I say.

"Funny," she says. "Now go tell her you're all right."

I walk out of my parents' bedroom and into the living room, where Elinor is sitting with her coat and backpack on. I see that I have maybe ruined everything and I feel shaky. "You don't need to go home yet," I say. "I'm fine."

"Well, that's good, but I think I want to go home anyway. I think maybe astrology isn't your thing."

"Yes, it is! I just have some wacky thoughts sometimes, that's all. I love astrology already and I don't think it's hooey at all," I say. *Please, please, please don't go,* I think.

"Okay, well, good then. I really do hope the book helps you with the audition, but can your mom or dad take me home now?"

"I'll go get my dad," I say, and when I do they are gone very quickly out the door and all my perfect-new-best-friend dreams right along with them.

TAKE SEVEN

surprise guest stars, boys in bow ties, and butterflies over Broadway

This day has gone by so quickly, I haven't gotten to either of the things on the list I made during freewriting this morning — a list called *My Pre-Audition Fix-It List*:

1. Thank Charlotte for trying to help with the acting lesson.

2. Apologize over and over to Elinor for being a terrible new best friend.

"Okay, ev-er-ee-body," Ms. Leon says, standing up from her desk. "Let's gather our things and get ready for dee-smeesal." The classroom phone rings and all Ms. Leon says is "Mmm-hmm," and hangs it back up.

"Jules, honey," Ms. Leon says, looking my way over the rims of her rhinestone glasses, "please gather your things and go to the office."

Two things pop into my head at this moment: Either the principal found out that the mounds of dirt out by the playground were caused by me and my worm-excavation team and not by the mysterious giant groundhog he suspects, OR someone has died. The fact that Ms. Leon said *honey* leads me to believe that it is not the hole-digging option, but the death option.

On my way up to the front of the room, I picture myself at my mother's bedside in the hospital, sobbing, and then I think that I will probably not be able to go to my audition today, which is probably better, anyway.

"Did someone die?" I ask Ms. Leon as I turn my chair upside down and hoist it onto my desk.

"Ay, Jules, the drama!" she says. "No, someone did not die. You just have a special visitor here to pick you up."

My heart races. I absolutely know who it is and I run so fast out of the classroom that I forget my backpack and have to turn right back. Ay!

When I go back in the room for my backpack, it isn't Elinor or even Teddy who hands it to me. It is Charlotte. "Here you go, Jules," she says. "Break a leg!" I look at her kind of funny and say thanks, since I think this is a nice thing to say and not a terrible thing to say, but I don't get it.

"I sneaked a peek at your list this morning," she says. *Aha!* I think. "I told you how to guard your paper and you still don't do it.

Anyway, you're welcome," she says, and I am very, very happy that old-Charlotte showed up at this knee-quaking moment.

Grandma Gilda is waiting for me in the office and I practically knock her down when I hug her. "I didn't know you were picking me up, George!" I yell.

"Well, of course not," she says. "That would have ruined the surprise. Why are you calling me George?"

"I don't know. The idea just popped into my head on the way here," I say.

"Okay, I like it, Eddie," she says.

I smile. "I like it," I say.

We hustle across Broadway to catch the downtown bus. We are headed to Times Square — Times Square! When the bus

comes, we line up behind all the people who were waiting before us. I am face-to-face with a picture of a very snazzy-looking lady who I recognize from the news. I wonder if she always wanted to have her picture on the side of the M104 bus. In my head, I add *snazzy* to my signature-words list.

On the bus, I have butterflies in my stomach, which reminds me of the tropical butterflies at the Museum of Natural History. I picture myself letting all those flitting-around butterflies escape that hot, soggy room and I think how beautiful they would look flying in between city buildings, dodging American flags and neon signs flashing the words HOT COFFEE.

The bus screeches to a halt.

We hop down to the ground and I feel like I am going to throw up loads of butterflies all over Times Square. But I stop myself when I look at George. She thinks I could be a world-famous actress, and world-famous actresses definitely do not throw up butterflies in garbage cans.

"Listen, Eddie," George says when we are about to walk into a big building with a revolving door that looks like it's gobbling up one group of people and spitting out another right before my eyes. I can hardly blink.

"Eddie!" George says again, and I look at her. "This is just for fun, you know. Pretend you're in front of the mirror in your room, doing your fizzy ice-cream cone jingle for

Big Henry. And if you throw up, you throw
up! It'll be a funny story."

"Real funny," I say.

She gives me a Grandma Gilda–sized
squeeze, which is so tight it almost squeezes
all the butterflies out of me. Almost.

"Are you good?" she asks.

"Snazzy," I say.

"Snazzy?" George says.

"I'm trying it on," I say, and then I swallow hard and let the revolving door swallow
me up.

In the elevator, Grandma Gilda pulls out
a little velvet box and hands it to me.

"What's this?" I ask.

"The solution to your problem," she says.

I open the box.

"Earrings?" I say.

"Not just earrings," she says. "Magic ear-rings." I narrow my eyes at her.

"Fine, don't believe me," she says. "All I know is that every time they have ever been worn, they have brought magic with them."

"What kind of magic?" I ask, eyeing the little gold stars. I got my ears pierced for my sixth birthday and have never once taken out the earrings I got pierced with — they are little rubies, my birthstone.

"Magic like your mom being born, your uncle Michael being born, magic things like that," she says. I smile.

"Maybe if you wear them today, a star will be born." She says this in a tall-icy-drink kind of a voice and makes jazz hands at me. I am glad there is no one else in the elevator.

"Ha-ha, George," I say.

"Ha-ha, Eddie," she says.

I put the earrings on and hand Grandma my old ones.

When we walk inside the audition office, we find a roomful of kids. I am surprised that there are girls *and* boys. This makes things much worse for me. Here's why:

1. Boys can always talk loud and say whatever they want.

2. Boys are always funny, even when they are trying to be serious.

3. Boys don't get nervous, unless they are Teddy, but Teddy would never try out for a commercial in the first place.

For all of these reasons, I decide right away that a boy will end up in this

commercial, pretending to love the horrible orange-tasting mouthwash for all the world to see.

George sits down and holds my hand tight while we wait. And wait and wait and wait. I watch as the door opens and closes a million times and kid after kid gets called in before me by a woman with a clipboard. In my head, I picture each one of them on the Swish commercial and they all do it perfectly. They look like the kinds of kids who know what they are doing. They are wearing outfits that match from their headbands to their tights. One boy — and this is the boy I would hire for this particular job — is dressed in blue jeans, a pin-striped shirt, and a bow tie. He looks sharp. What was my mom thinking putting me in charge of dressing myself for this, anyway? I look down at my rainbow shoelaces and think I'm not at all perfect for this.

"Jules Bloom!" someone yells.

"Off you go," Grandma Gilda says.

I take one of Charlotte's for-real-acting-lesson deep breaths and follow the woman with the clipboard.

"Hi, Jules," Colby Kingston says to me from behind a camera. "It's good to see you."

"It's good to be here," I say. I had decided earlier that I was going to try to talk in complete sentences at this audition, since it sounds so nice on Elinor.

"Have a seat," she says.

I sit down at a little white sink with a big bottle of Swish and a stack of little paper cups on it. As if someone might want to taste Swish over and over again. I feel my knees get shaky.

"Are you ready, honey?" Colby Kingston asks me.

"Mmm-hmm," I say. "I mean, yes, I'm ready."

"So, when the director says *action*, you say your lines. Got it?"

"Got it," I say.

"And . . . action," I hear. Here goes nothing.

"Swishing is my favorite part of the day," I say into the camera in my best jingle voice.

"It's a little bit sweet, a little bit minty, and a whole lot of fun," I say. I am thinking that this isn't going to be so bad. I even like how I sound.

"And who wouldn't love that orange-fresh taste?" I ask the camera, picking up that tiny cup full of gross. "Have you Swished today?" I say.

I stare at the orange liquid for what is probably a little too long, then I close my eyes, and into my mouth it goes. I swish it around just like I am supposed to, and I am okay for exactly one second, until I feel the sticky orange lump in my throat. I try everything I can to keep the swish going for just one more second. I even think of Charlotte telling me to focus, and I do — I really do.

I puff out my cheeks, thinking maybe *that* will keep the orange grossness away from my taste buds. Then I think of Teddy and I realize that I don't even mind the smell of the orange today. His spray worked. But the taste — oh! I can't take it. I touch my earrings. If they are so magical, why do I feel like I am going to . . . to . . .

I spit the orange stuff all over — my mouth is like a fountain. There is no throw up, but there is orange mouthwash every-where. I feel bubbles of it on my tongue and my lips.

Everyone is watch-ing me. I am about to cry or run away, but then I think of Elinor. I decide to go with it. I smile, wipe off my mouth with my sleeve, and I sing.

"That's how you make a fizzy ice-cream cone / That's how you do it / That's how you do it." I belt this out at the top of my lungs and I even get up and do a little twirl like I would do if I were in my living room. "Cha-cha-cha!" I add at the end, just for a little more pizzazz.

The room is silent and my face gets hot. *At least it is over*, I think.

But then I hear clapping. It is Colby Kingston. She comes over to me and pats my shoulder. "Wow, Jules. That was really something. You are really something."

"Sorry about that," I say. "I'm not much of an orange person."

"Maybe not, but the camera sure loves you," she says, bending down and putting her hands on my shoulders. My stomach flips when she says this. Good butterflies. "I'm going to call your mom in a little bit, after these last auditions. Okay?"

"Okay," I say. "Thanks."

I walk out into the waiting room and find Grandma Gilda reading a magazine.

"Hey, George," I say. "You aren't even pacing."

"Hey, Eddie," she says. "I have other things to do besides worry about you throwing up on camera."

I laugh.

"So?" she asks.

"So," I say, "I didn't throw up, but I did spit the mouthwash all over the place and then I started singing my fizzy-milk jingle and I even danced and said *cha-cha-cha* at the end."

"*Cha-cha-cha* is always a good idea," she says.

"I thought so," I say.

TAKE EIGHT

crying cats and dogs, blackout barbecues, and secrets of the not-Swish girl

We take the elevator down to the lobby and let the revolving door spit us back out onto the street.

"Well, you did it!" Grandma Gilda says now, scooping me up and swinging me around in the almost-night.

"Did what?" I say, laughing.

"You made it through your first audition, and you didn't give up when it didn't go just right, either. You improvised. Wow."

"What's *improvise*?" I ask.

"It's when you just go with something, even if it wasn't what you had planned to do," she says. I smile and think of Elinor. Thank goodness we are opposites. I never would have thought of that idea on my own.

We take a taxi home and I let my hand hang out the window so I can feel the air. It starts to drizzle a little and I feel some tears come up through my throat and into my eyes. "Go ahead and cry, Julesie," Grandma says. "You must be relieved."

I cry and cry for a couple minutes, maybe
because I know I am not going to be the
Swish girl and maybe because it's all over
and I don't have to be nervous anymore. By
the time we get to 91st Street, it is raining
cats and dogs, but my tears are all dried up.

We hustle out of the cab and hold hands as we run to the building, covering our heads.

I stop right before we open the door to my apartment because I am going to have to tell my parents and Big Henry that I am no Swish girl.

"Go on, Eddie," George says. "This isn't going to be as hard as you think."

I open the door and all the lights are out, and I think for a second that there is a blackout, and then I get excited and picture my whole family around a pretend campfire made out of a pile of flashlights, eating s'mores and telling ghost stories that are more funny than scary by the flashlight fire.

But no, it is not a blackout at all.

"Surprise!" The lights come on and I see my mom and my dad and Big Henry and Ugly Otis and Teddy and Charlotte and Elinor, and they are all wearing party hats and my dad is holding a big, beautiful cake that has a line down the middle. On one side it says *Way to Go!* and on the other it says *Best Try Ever!*

I am definitely surprised. "We're going to have to eat the Best Try Ever section," I say.

"You threw up?" Teddy asks, his eyes popping out of his head.

"I knew it," Charlotte says, "I knew it when she said her favorite food was meatballs."

"I didn't throw up," I yell, interrupting everyone. "I just . . . spit up. But then I sang my jingle and I danced and I *cha-cha-cha*ed and Colby Kingston clapped and said I was something. And even though I know that *something* probably means that she thinks I am crazy and not at all the right girl to be the Swish girl, I still think she liked me and that I wasn't totally and completely horrible." I take a deep breath. "I just went with it," I say, looking at Elinor, who smiles a big smile at me, and I am so happy that she is the kind of person who shows up for a party for a person who was such a jerk the day before.

"Yay!" Big Henry cheers. And then he runs toward me and before I know it, he has tackled me with a giant Big Henry hug and we are on the floor, which is where I always end up when Big Henry is involved.

Everyone is laughing all around me and my parents are clapping and I feel very happy.

But then the phone rings. "Get it," I shout at my mom from underneath my brother. I stand up and pull Big Henry up with me.

She hurries to the phone and says, "Hello, home of the not–Swish girl." I almost fall back down when she does this.

"Oh, hi, Colby. Yes, Jules was just telling us all about it. Mmm-hmm . . . okaaay . . . really?" I watch and listen and I feel Elinor take my hand and then I feel Charlotte take my other hand and I am surprised that

Starlight Cafe,

Robot

Just Good Food

Palate

Red PAINT

Charlotte does this but then I am even more surprised when Teddy takes Charlotte's hand and she doesn't throw Teddy out the window.

We all just stand and wait, holding hands in a row like we are waiting for Red Rover to come and knock us all over.

"Well, sure, I don't know. Sounds interesting," my mom says. "Yep, will do. Thanks so much." And *click*, the call is over.

I let go of the Red Rover line and cover my ears.

"You are going to want to hear this, Jules."

I take my hands away and close my eyes instead.

"So," she says, "you didn't get the commercial. But —"

"But what?" Charlotte yells.

"They want you to be in a movie."

"A what?" I say, opening my eyes wide.

"A movie. A spy movie, actually," my mom says, shaking her head.

The room is silent.

"Jules is going to be a star?" Charlotte asks.

"I don't know," my dad says. "Is that what Jules wants?"

I am speechless, like the night I met Colby Kingston. Everyone is looking at me.

I raise my hand and my mom smiles at me.

"Yes, Jules," my mom says.

"Mrs. Bloom, do I have to eat something orange in the movie?"

"I doubt it," my mom says.

"Smell something orange?"

"I don't think so."

"Wear something orange?"

"Jules."

"Then, yes," I say. "I think I would like to be a star."

"Let's start with a small part in a spy movie and see where we go, okay?"

"Okay!"

Then we all cheer and we eat cake and I don't even picture myself doing anything else other than this.

This is better than pretend.

It is late at night and I can hear Paddington through the curtain. I have a new list to make. *Secrets of the Not–Swish Girl* (I am practicing being secretive for the spy movie):

1. I am secretly glad that I am not the Swish girl and that the pinstripe-and-bow-tie-wearing boy is the new face of Swish Mouthwash for Kids. (I was right!)

2. I am also secretly happy that it rained so much today because Charlotte told me that in the movies, something dramatic always happens when it rains, and it did! I got a part in a real Hollywood movie! Charlotte was right! And the rain also means that the worms will come now and there will be water

overflowing in their swimming pool so they will make giganto-huge splashes when they fly off the high-dive and it will be just like in the movies. All around, people will cheer (even new-Charlotte), and the birds will chirp, and the flowers will bloom —

I stop writing, put my pen down, and run into the living room. "I've got it!" I yell.

"You've got what?" my dad asks. He and my mom are still cleaning up the not-the-new-Swish-girl party. I walk over to the can of red paint and dip the brush in it. There is a wide-open spot on the wall and I use it all. In the biggest letters I know how to make, I write *BLOOM!* Just like that. With an exclamation point.

My dad stands up and picks me up. "I love it," he says.

"It's perfect, Jules," my mom says.

I let them hug me for a while because it feels so nice and because it means I am staying up even later, which means writing on the wall is an even better way to put off bedtime than the Great Toothbrush Challenge.

And then I say, "Good, now that that's settled, let's talk about the menu. I'm thinking minty-chocolate candies ought to be served with everything."

"I'm thinking you and your minty-fresh thoughts ought to get back into bed," my mom says.

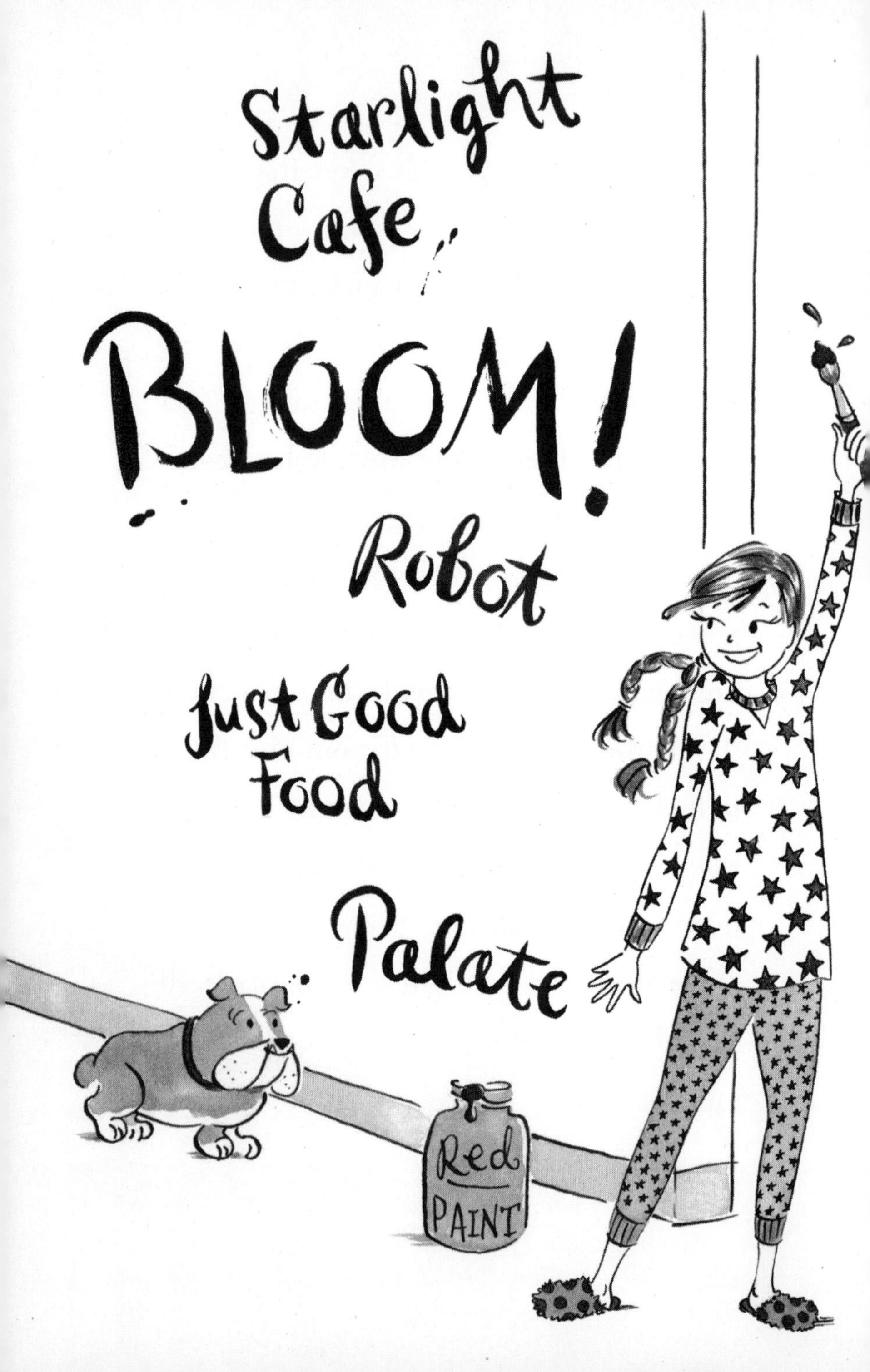
Starlight Cafe
BLOOM!
Robot
Just Good Food
Palate
Red PAINT

"Minty-fine idea," I say.

"Good night, Jules," my dad says.

"Good night, Mr. and Mrs. Bloom," I say. "Thanks for letting me be . . . well, letting me be me."

"Thanks for being you," my mom says.

"You're welcome," I say.

I hop into my room, but I peek back around the corner and listen to what my parents say. I have to strain to hear their whispers. What's that? Did I hear them say that doing this spy movie means no camp this summer? I do a silent song and dance in the dark. Ooh, I think love spying already . . .

The End

For a sneak peek at Jules's
next starring role, turn the page!

★ ★ ★

STARRING Jules

(IN DRAMA-RAMA)

Lights!

Camera!

Action!

There is nothing better than the few seconds before an announcement. Ms. Leon will probably just say that we are supposed to bring in all box tops by Friday, but for this one second before she says that, I picture the word ANNOUNCEMENT all lit up behind Ms. Leon, and then I picture her saying, *"Charlotte Pinkerton, you've learned all you can for this year, so pack up your backpack and we'll see you next year!"* I know very well she won't say this, but at least for a few seconds I get to pretend the announcement has nothing at all to do with box tops.

"I have decided that for this year's moving-up ceremony we will put on a little show. *¡Un espectáculo!*"

An idea pops right into my head and

comes flying out of my mouth as I shoot my hand in the air. "I want to be the director!" This is the first time in my whole life I have ever raised my hand without making extra sure I knew exactly what would come out of my mouth.

I feel everyone's eyes on me, but especially Charlotte's. "I am surprised to hear this, Jules!" Ms. Leon says. "I thought you were a budding actress."

"I am," I say, my face heating up the way it does. "But, I think I would like this, too."

"Thank you for telling me, but we'll figure it out tomorrow. For now, we write!"

We all pull out our notebooks and I have a list written as fast as ever, guarding my paper the way Charlotte showed me so she will not see one single word.

Reasons Why I Should Be the Director of the Moving-Up-Ceremony Show:

1. I would get to boss Charlotte and the ABC's around.

2. I would get to make Elinor hoot and holler for real so she will not be sad-serious anymore — top-secret mission accomplished!

3. I would not have to act in front of my whole class and their whole families, since the entire idea of speaking in front of people I actually know makes me more nauseous than orange mouthwash.

ACKNOWLEDGMENTS

Most anyone who knows me will also know that Jules and Big Henry bear very close resemblance to Grace and Elijah Ain. While this is true, and while I would not have come up with one sentence of this book without them, the two of them are truly unto themselves. I could never capture the intelligence, the wit, or the imagination they bring to their every experience. Not to mention the extraordinary joy and pride they bring me every day. Thank you both for being so authentically you.

And while my own husband spends his day in a corporate office and not cooking up the organic meals (nor writing that Great

American Novel) of his dreams, he is in so many ways my Robby Bloom, inspiring me every day with his curiosity, his extraordinary fathering, and his pursuit of life. His support is one of the great blessings of my life.

To the people who read this, over and over until it was ready, I thank you for your feedback and encouragement. That means you, Gail Levine, and you, Kelli Novak, and you, Chava Ortner. To the kids and parents of the JCC of Manhattan Class of 2010 for inspiring this book in the first place. To my first-ever kid reader, and occasional digger of worms, Lia Ortner, who gave me the confidence to submit this at long last, thank you, thank you!

To Jenne Abramowitz and Abby McAden, thank you for loving Jules, for giving her a home where she is understood, and for bringing her out into the daylight with such gusto. And to Jill Grinberg, for believing in me in a way I still can't believe myself, I am grateful beyond words.

BETH AIN was raised in Allentown, PA, but fell in love with New York City, where she lived until recently and where she even tried her hand at raising two kids, an experience that gave her some good lessons in what makes city kids (and city moms) tick. Enter Jules Bloom—lover of all things Upper West Side. In search of wide-open spaces, Beth headed for the hills of Port Washington, Long Island, where she, her husband, and their two kids have fallen in love all over again. This time with small-town life, where thankfully, she can see the Empire State Building from Main Street, which makes it pretty easy to imagine what Jules is up to over there.

31901051915660